Ashna, a boy of ancient Sumeria, thinks of a way to improve the log rollers that move the sledges. Everyone is pleased, for now one ox can do the work of two. And when fierce tribesmen attack the Sumerian city, Ashna's "fast roller" helps win a victory for his people.

by Chester G. Osborne

The First Wheel

ILLUSTRATED BY RICHARD N. OSBORNE

Follett Publishing Company *Chicago*

OTHER BOOKS BY CHESTER G. OSBORNE

The First Puppy

The First Bow and Arrow

The First Lake Dwellers

Library of Congress Catalog Card Number: 59-10273

Preface

In the beginning man had but his brain, his power of speech, and his two hands with which to conquer his world. In Mr. Osborne's first book, we were told how the discovery of the bow and arrow helped man assure his survival. Then came the tale of how animals were domesticated and put to the service of their human masters. Next we read of life during the first of the economic revolutions sketched by one of the world's greatest archaeologists, the late V. Gordon Childe, whereby man took the next step in assuring the continuance of his society by learning to grow, rather than to gather, his food.

With this book, we reach the next stage, the second of the great revolutions in human culture, when man built towns and cities, and society became organized into the stable political units we call states. Here, in ancient Sumer, we find a people who had writing, could read, knew arithmetic, and engaged in trade.

But a better standard of living, the arts of reading and writing and arithmetic, only brought on new problems. Organized warfare came when the riches men accumulated aroused the envy of others, and to protect their wealth they barricaded themselves behind town walls; with trade came raiding; the need for workers gave rise to slavery. And as it was long before Sumer existed and until today, men ventured into the dangerous places for the love of adventure, and for their gain.

Always, too, there has been the independent thinker, the inventor, the intellectual adventurer, for these are the stuff out of which change in civilization is made. In each of Mr. Osborne's books it is the lad of intelligence and courage who is the hero. Here, Ashna combines the inventive genius that gives his people the wheel with the courage to brave their disfavor when he dares to defy the law which held that an escaping slave might not be helped even when it was a question of preserving life. He represents something else new in man's experience — the humanitarian, whose behavior is based on sympathy and understanding for those who are deprived of the advantages others possess.

The moral is clear; it is the dissenters of today who become the prophets of tomorrow. And we, like the Sumerians, are coming to realize that our salvation may lie in our hearkening to those adventurers of the mind who, because we disagree with them, we would reject.

MELVILLE J. HERSKOVITS

Department of Anthropology
Northwestern University

The First Wheel

Bandits Attack the Rafts

1

Thunder rolled over the small city in northern Sumeria. In the gray gloom of dawn, lightning flared over the great temple, the walls, and little mud-brick houses.

In the home of Essna, an official of the city, a twelve-year-old boy named Ashna pushed aside a window cover and stared out into the storm. The drum and splash of hoofbeats came clearly into the dimly lighted room.

"A man is hurrying down the street. He comes here," the boy said. He was a slender boy with dark, intense eyes and touseled black hair. He spoke to his older sister, Ti'amat, a girl slightly taller than he.

They looked out. The rider glanced back over his shoulder; he bent low, kicked hard at the onager, the long-eared steed he rode, and went faster.

A moment later the rider was thumping at the door. "Essna!" he shouted. "It is I, Mashkim. They follow me!"

Ashna let him in. "I will call my father."

"Bring him right away. Bandits are attacking the rafts!" The stout man pushed past Ashna. He was wet, and his plump face was white above his beard.

The rafts were essential to the city, the boy knew. They would be carrying food, livestock, ores, and wood, and their very frames would be needed for weapons and building.

"I hear, Mashkim." Essna strode in, gray-haired and grim-faced in the yellow light of the oil lamp. "Where are the rafts?"

"The head raft is stuck in a shallows where the canal flows into the Tigris River." Mashkim's shaky hands brushed at his face. "Our men and supplies dangle from that sandbar like fish on a hook. The bandits shoot at them from the eastern shore.

8

"Your sons sent me ashore. My onager and I swam half the width of the river." His fat lips were loose with fear. "I think I was followed."

Essna flung the door open briefly. Rain whipped in. "The street is empty," he said calmly. "I will send my son Ashna for the guards at the temple. You will find dry robes in that room. My daughter Ti'amat and Nin, my wife, will bring you a warm drink."

As Ti'amat and Nin hurried to help Mashkim, Ashna tied on his cloak and picked up a javelin. His father said, "Tell the guards what you heard. I will get my onager and meet them at the gate."

"Is it safe to send the boy?" Nin, his mother, asked. "If the enemy did follow Mashkim, they may be lurking outside."

Ashna hesitated. At dawn, the wide gates to the plain would be open and unattended, as was the custom except in time of war. Essna said, "The river is a great barrier. The attack is from the other shore. The bandits would find it nearly impossible to cross."

"Essna may be right," the stout man admitted. "In the storm, every thorn bush seemed to hide a spirit."

"Go now," Essna said to Ashna.

9

The boy ran out. Lightning crackled. The wind whistled in the reedy roofs of the houses. He ran faster. As he passed the open gate of the city, lightning brightened the distant plains. Ashna caught a glimpse of a rider galloping away. So Mashkim had been followed!

Ashna bounded up the long stairway to the temple. A sentinel met him. Over the crash of thunder, the boy gave the message.

In a few moments, men were gathering at the gate. Torches blazed and hissed in the rain. The guards came with weapons and long coils of rope.

THE FIRST WHEEL

Essna rode up. "You who have mounts will ride to the end of the canal. Those on foot will follow with teams of oxen; Mashkim will lead them."

Ashna told Essna about the rider on the plain. Essna frowned. "One of the bandits may have crossed, then. But our whole city is out in force now; one thief will not worry us.

"Go back and help Mashkim," he told Ashna. The boy glanced enviously at the guards with their fleet little onagers. "Get our oxen," Essna was saying.

The troop clattered away. Ashna ran back. In the stable, his sister hauled some heavy yokes down from their hooks. Mashkim prodded the oxen. "They will not arise. Our men dangle in the river!"

"I can get them up," the boy said. Soon he led them out into the storm.

"Hurry!" Mashkim begged. He mounted his onager.

"Ashna hates to use a whip, even now," Ti'amat said, with a trace of anger in her voice. "But I will stir these sluggish beasts. Yo! Get along!" She lashed at them.

"Not too fast," Ashna warned. "If the oxen slip in this mud, we shall never get there in time."

At the gate the rest of the guard joined them. Crowds

of men and women followed, for the report of danger had spread fast; everyone understood that in the desolate plains of Sumeria, the city's life depended on its transportation and waterways.

"Make the oxen run," Ti'amat insisted. "Sint and Lugud are on those rafts. Oh, hurry!" The boy prodded the oxen. Beside them, the people broke into a run.

At the river they saw the rafts stretching toward the far bank; over there, dim figures rode back and forth.

Mashkim groaned. "We cannot touch the bandits, but they can hit the men on the last raft."

"Stand away!" Essna called to Sint and Lugud on the rafts. "Here is a line!" Essna fitted an arrow with a coil of string winding away from its head. "Watch out," he yelled. The arrow arched up.

"Too far," Ashna whispered. "The arrow passes over."

But Lugud leaped up and seized the string. Essna tied a strong rope to his end, and Lugud carefully pulled the string hand over hand. The rope snaked its way out; Lugud grasped it, and Sint tied it securely.

"Hitch this end to the ox teams," Essna shouted to Mashkim and Ashna. "Turn the oxen."

They obeyed. The oxen strained. The rope tightened. The first raft slid over the sandbar, and the others followed. The onlookers cheered and yelled in relief.

BANDITS ATTACK THE RAFTS

"Now to the canal. Haul them to the city!" Essna ordered.

Someone shouted, "The bandits are giving up — they ride away!"

Carefully Mashkim and Ashna led the oxen along the river bank. As each raft came close, the guards threw out more lines. The leading raft swung into the canal. There the water ran fast and deep because of the months of rain, and Sint and Lugud and their crews used long poles to keep their rafts from crashing against the embankment.

Where the waterway passed the city, Ashna and Mashkim stopped. Here the rafts would unload. A man who had been wounded earlier in the fight was helped ashore.

Sint and Lugud ran to greet Ashna and the others. They were glad to have reached home after their dangerous trip.

"You managed the oxen very well," Sint told his youngest brother. Sint was tall and slender, with eyes as dark and sharp as Ashna's; the two looked very much alike. Lugud was heavier; he could hurl a spear with deadlier aim than anyone in the city. For a time he had been in the temple guard, and fighting was almost a trade with him.

The boy gazed with interest at the rafts. "You brought more onagers!"

"We did, but they are for the temple," Sint replied.

"They were very expensive," Lugud said. He and Sint knew what their younger brother was thinking. Ashna had always wanted a mount of his own.

Essna said briskly, "Boys do not have onagers. Now there is more work. You and your sister will untie the goat-skin floats on the rafts. Flatten them, tie them in bundles, and keep a good account."

As Ashna and Ti'amat began, there was great activity all around them. Other ox teams plodded up. Workmen called noisily. The guards brought a group of slaves and stood nearby with whips and spears.

Ashna untied the goatskin bags. There were many of them, fastened to the sides; they were filled with air to help keep the rafts afloat. Ti'amat let the air out and pressed them down with her hands.

As each stack grew, Ashna made a total; he used a tablet of clay and made marks with a reed stylus. Once he paused to watch as the last of the onagers were loaded with packs and brought ashore. The animals kicked and brayed in fright as the rafts rocked under their hooves.

15

When there were more than a hundred bags counted, Ti'amat said that she wanted to take them in. "I have had enough of the rain," she complained. "I am wet. My fingers ache from the cold and from pulling at these strings." She looked around for her father.

"A slave will take the bags," Essna called. He beckoned to a youth not much older than Ashna. The slave walked toward the raft.

Suddenly the youth turned about and ran. He bounded to an empty raft. A guard shouted in alarm, "He tries to escape!"

"He may get across the canal," Essna said. "No one is there to halt him. After him!"

The slave made a desperate jump from the raft. But the canal was too wide in that place. He reached out, then plunged into the deep water. His arms thrashed.

Essna said, "Let him go."

Ti'amat cried, "Oh, the slave cannot swim. The current takes him."

Ashna dashed to the shore. But a guard swung a spear in front of him. "Stay here, boy. The slaves are rebellious. There is a law. We will do nothing."

Ashna stared in horror. The slave bobbed up and

16

down. Steadily the current pulled him down the canal, past the next raft.

All the workmen stopped. There was a sudden quiet. Ti'amat moaned. "He is being carried down to the Tigris. He is drowning."

Ashna stepped sideways, away from the guard and the spear. Then he darted through the throng of workmen, toward the end raft.

He bounded to the deck, glanced quickly around, loosened a mooring rope, and flung it out over the water.

17

It fell in front of the slave. He seized it, and Ashna hauled him in.

The slave clutched at the deck, gasping for breath. But he was alive.

"Ashna, you should not have done that." Lugud stepped briskly to the raft. He dragged the slave to his feet and shoved him to the waiting guards. "You should not have done that," he repeated. "The guard told you."

"I thought but to help," Ashna began to say.

His father rode up. "Back to the house, Ashna." His voice was loud and severe. "We will talk of this later."

Ti'amat said nothing, for she was stunned. But as the boy walked slowly past Sint, he heard his older brother whisper, "Father is not as angry as he seems. Soon you will understand. Now go, as he said."

A Trip Up the Euphrates

2

From the window of his home, Ashna saw the cargoes brought through the gate. Men shouted. Whips lashed. Oxen bellowed and strained at the long sledges. Onagers trotted nimbly by, their lighter burdens lashed to dragging poles. Up the temple steps, slaves carried sacks to the food storage bins.

"I would rather work than stand here," Ashna said to his mother.

"Other boys and girls do not work," Nin replied. "See, they stand around the temple steps or run after the sledges, playing and shouting."

"Most of the others have had no education. I have been to the school at the temple. I can read and write and do arithmetic. I can keep accounts." He turned his face away. "I was doing that when I got into trouble."

Nin said patiently, "I did not see what happened. But your father is an official. He can explain. He will. You may not be punished any more.

"Now we are pleased that Sint and Lugud are home after a month away," she continued. "Our family must give thanks; place this fruit before our shrine, as an offering."

The boy took a bowl of dried dates and figs to the shrine. This was a tiny clay figure set in a niche in the wall. It had been in the house ever since the boy could remember. It was the god of wisdom. Its gray face had wide, popping eyes.

"What mistake did I make?" the boy asked silently. The wide eyes of the figure glared at him.

A noise from the street cut into his thought. A load of limestone blocks was being hauled to the temple. The load stopped. Two men came around from the rear with a log roller and laid it in front. As the load went over this, it rolled across others, which were in their turn brought

20

forward again for continual use.

Someone shouted. "One log rolls crookedly. The blocks slide. Look out!"

A large stone slid toward the ground. Men dodged

away. One man was not fast enough. The block fell on his leg. He cried out in pain.

Sint came, yelling an order. Ashna started forward, but remembered that he must stay indoors.

At Sint's call, several slaves thrust a log under the stone and pried it up. The man cried out again, but he was free. He rolled aside, clutching at his leg, until a pair of men carried him away.

Sint ordered a new log to be shoved under the sledge. Soon it was rumbling forward again.

It was dark before all the cargoes were unloaded. Then in Essna's house there was a feast, as Nin had promised. There was milk-and-barley soup, roast salmon, roast pig, wheat bread, cheese, and fruit. As Ti'amat and Nin brought the food in, Sint and Lugud were loud in their praise of it. But Ashna was silent.

"You had better speak to the boy," Sint whispered to his father. "He does not understand. He is too unhappy to eat."

"We are not very angry with you, although we made it seem that way in front of the crowd at the canal." Essna chose his words carefully. "Indeed, we need all the slaves.

"But the assembly has passed a law: a slave who

escapes may be punished by death if he is caught. The law is an answer to the tribesmen of the mountain regions; in their land, some Sumerians are held captives just as we hold these slaves, and they, too, are killed if they try to escape."

"Sumerians cannot show themselves weaker than others," Sint added. "The tribesmen, the desert nomads, the bandits, all must respect us. Each has his own law. But they have one thing in common: they would attack the city and destroy us if they thought they could."

Ashna said, "But you trade with those people. And they come here — "

"We have an uneasy peace," Essna admitted. "There are border fights. Men are killed or captured. But as yet there is no war. Our city assembly does not want that."

"We have to put up with the bandit raids," Sint explained, "while we keep up trade for the things our city needs. Trade and transport are like life's blood to the city. The longer we can delay a real war, the stronger our city will grow, and the better chance we will have to win."

Lugud grumbled. "I do not agree with all of this. We are hard on the slaves, but we do not fight back. We are not too weak to send out a war party; we could go after those bandits of last night, for example."

Essna said, "Enough talk. Now Ashna understands that Sumerians must at least appear to be as rough and violent as the outsiders are, and he knows of the law about slaves."

"Tell him what we talked about this afternoon," Sint said. "Then perhaps he will forget that slave trouble and eat."

"There will be another trip soon. But because the slaves are rebellious, only Sumerians will go, and the caravan will be short of men. Extra help is needed.

"I cannot go, for the rains will soon end, and I must manage the canal construction.

"Your brothers want you to go with them as a scribe and accountant. The temple would pay you with a small amount of silver for your work; that would be all, since you could not increase your earnings with private trading as the other crewmen do.

"The trip will be up the Euphrates River to find a new trade route. It will not be easy. There may be danger." Essna glanced at Nin. She hesitated and then nodded slightly.

"You have our permission to go."

Ashna's eyes sparkled. Pay or not, this would be exciting. A new trade route! To go with Sint and Lugud! Ti'amat clapped her hands in her happiness for him. Sint said, "Now our younger brother is too excited to eat. But we are not. Come, lad, eat with us!"

And Ashna did.

The caravan formed a few days later. Ashna and Sint made lists of the supplies. They wrote on clay tablets, and as each tablet was finished, it was wrapped in another, thinner sheet of clay to protect the writing.

The men fastened their packs. Each onager had a burden on its back and another slung across a pair of dragging poles.

"Count the weapons," said Sint. "And each man must have camping gear and food for his own use. Nothing can be forgotten."

To a man with an ox, Sint said, "Too slow. No oxen this time. We must return before the river falls in the summer drought."

A priest in scarlet robes spoke to Sint and directed that some of the temple stores be added to the packs. Sint had to speak to still another man. "No riders. Except for the scouts, everyone will walk."

Mashkim objected. "I can take enough on drag poles."

But Sint was firm. When the last traveler had taken his place, Sint frowned and said, "I thought there would be more."

"Twenty men and twenty onagers." Ashna was quick with figures. "I counted twenty bows, four hundred arrows — "

"There were more than twenty bandits on the Tigris," Sint interrupted. "I'll ask the priest for some guards."

The men waited impatiently. One muttered angrily when his packs slipped. Mashkim sulked. Ashna took the time to run to Nin and Ti'amat for a few last words.

At last Sint returned. "It is too close to planting season. The guards must stay with the slaves in the fields."

"I, too, would stay and plant," said the tall, thin man called Babbir.

"Take some men with oxen," Nagar the carpenter said. "We refuse them, yet we so load our onagers that they crawl."

"They will not crawl for long," Sint said. "At Hit we can leave a part of our cargo, and on the way back we can pick up what is owed us. We can ride the timber rafts which we will build in the mountain country."

A bearded man named Utul said, "The traders at Hit are all thieves. I know them. They will take everything and give nothing."

"You should know about the thieves at Hit." Nagar laughed. "You are related to everyone there, are you not?"

Utul shook his fist. Someone whooped with joy, expecting a fight. But Lugud, who had been waiting quietly, rode up to the men. "You bark like jackals, and with no more sense," he snapped. "We are under orders of the city assembly, and of the temple. We have temple supplies in our packs. We need them.

"Sint leads us." His face grew red. "Now if any man question Sint further, I, Lugud, will toss him on my spear though he may howl like a jackal, and I will fling him into the canal."

The men became silent. As Lugud turned his onager away, Utul said to Nagar, "You were right, I must admit. I have a brother-in-law who is a thief, I think. But is he not your cousin?" At that, all the men laughed.

When everything was ready, Sint mounted his onager. The caravan filed out through the city gate.

Ashna slid his javelin into the straps on the animal he

led and tied the bag of clay tablets to the poles. He turned for a last look. Ti'amat and Nin waved silently from the house. He waved back. As he did so, his heart pounded. This would be a difficult trip. It might be a month or longer before he would see his family again.

THE FIRST WHEEL

Sint cantered past to lead the group. Lugud, heavy
and broad-shouldered, rode far ahead as a scout. "They
know what to do," Ashna thought. "I will be safe with
them."

Babbir Disappears

3

Westward went the caravan, past an orchard which the temple tried to grow on the treeless plain, through a marsh where slaves made irrigation ditches, past boys who fished in a canal. They looked enviously at Ashna, for he was the only boy on the trip.

The city wall faded. There was a light mist, but for a long time Ashna could see the black shape of the temple against the cloudy sky. At dusk they camped.

The next day they turned north along the Euphrates.

"The path is flooded," Lugud reported.

Sint rode out to see. "We can pass. But where the

river enters the canal, there is a cave-in. Essna should know."

"The river won't be high for long," Babbir said. "The rainy season is almost over."

Sint said, "The break could grow quickly. It could lower the canal level so that we could not float our rafts through when we come back. We must tell Essna."

Utul protested, "We can spare no one, unless we send the boy."

"Can you read and write?" Lugud asked. And when Utul shook his head, Lugud went on, "The boy can. That is why he is with us. He may save many of us from being cheated in the market places."

"The boy stays. I will tell Essna." Babbir unpacked his onager. "I may catch up to you tomorrow." The lanky trader galloped away.

Nagar worried. "One man less."

"All his packs must be carried," Mashkim grumbled. "Where can we put them?"

"We cannot leave them here. The sky darkens. It is going to rain again," Utul declared.

"We'll make a sledge from the drag poles." Sint said to Ashna, "Bring your onager."

He laced the poles together. Mashkim was doubtful. "The poles are not strong enough. Four packs must go on; there were two, and now there are Babbir's."

"Test the sledge," Sint said. Ashna obeyed. The front end dug into the ground.

"You made a fine plow," Nagar grunted. He sat down.

"Tighten the harness," said Sint, "so that it lifts some of the weight off the front." Ashna did, but the onager kicked the sledge over.

"The harness chokes him," said Lugud. "Onagers cannot haul like oxen."

"But no one can carry the packs, and we must be free to scout," Sint replied. "If I could make rollers — "

Nagar hooted. "Then we would travel no faster than a snail."

"There is a way to peg the rollers. Nagar, bring your raft-building tools. Cut this, the thickest pole, for rollers. Mark its width. Then we will drill holes through the sledge and drive pegs past the rolling pieces."

"What will the pegs do?" Ashna asked.

"They will keep the rollers from slipping out." Ashna saw that Sint was planning to put pegs both in front and in back of the rollers, for he and Nagar bored eight holes.

Utul groaned. "Oh, open the packs. Divide them."

"You would complain of the extra weight a few moments later. No, we will finish this sledge." When the pegs were in place, Sint said, "Try that."

Ashna led the onager forward. The rollers rubbed and squeaked with the friction of the pegs, but the sledge moved. The caravan started. Sometimes the sledge hit bumps so that the rollers slipped down and out. Then Ashna had to stop and pry the roller back into the pegs. But the sledge would have to serve until Babbir returned.

At midday Lugud rode in. "There are rafts on the river. You will see them where the road turns."

"Bandits!" Mashkim said in alarm.

"Bandits do not build rafts," Sint assured him. But he ordered the travelers to hide in a clump of date palms.

As the rafts passed, Ashna could see their crews. Lugud ventured near enough to shout, "Who are you? Where do you go?"

The crewmen were startled. They raised their weapons. "We carry cargo to Ur, far down the river," was the answer.

"Sumerians." Sint's men came forward to talk to the raft crews. "What is it like upstream? Are there villages near this road?"

"We can find villages," Mashkim blurted. "Were there robbers?"

Sint repeated the question. The rafts were moving in a strong current, and he barely heard the reply: savage tribesmen had been seen beyond Hit, on the eastern shore.

The rafts vanished around a turn. Utul said, "On the eastern shore — that is this side!"

"We should turn back," someone said. "Or we could wait here for Babbir — we need him."

"Babbir deserts us," Mashkim declared. "Right now he may sit in his house, while we trudge on through the rain. My feet are blistered."

Lugud said to him, "We can change places. I will lead your onager. You can ride mine — and scout."

"I couldn't do that!" Mashkim said hastily.

"We go on now." Sint was firm. "The tribesmen may be friendly. We may be able to trade for more onagers."

At Hit, they made camp outside the city wall. Sint and Ashna went in to arrange to buy asphalt for the return trip. The others worked on new drag poles, for the old ones were worn and split.

A day later they went on. There was still no sign of Babbir, though the men watched constantly for him. At two villages they traded some bulky bags of feed for small, uncut precious stones. Now they could ride. Because the sledge had proved convenient for hauling the packs of tools and trading goods, they kept it in use.

They went far; their food supplies shrank so that they had to make camp earlier each day, in order to save time for hunting and fishing. Sint made maps on clay; he marked the changes in the river to use in guiding the rafts later on.

One day Lugud asked him to mark a place where the

river banks were high and where a line of shallows and flat stones showed a crossing. Here, Lugud observed, they should guard against an ambush.

Sint made a moon sign on the map.

"A sign of good luck?" Ashna asked, for Enzu, a moon god, was also the god of their city temple.

"No, although we could use the luck," Sint said, with a laugh. "The moon is my reminder to approach this place at night, if I can."

Lugud rolled up in a blanket. "We have had bad luck so far. The men are restless. The canal breaks. Babbir disappears. Now we enter a country of wild tribesmen."

"The men are indeed restless," Sint admitted. "They complain. They quarrel. They are rough. They complain so much that sometimes I think they enjoy it. But I think that they are loyal to us and to the city. We will get through."

"In this land, one must be rough to survive," Lugud said grimly.

Ashna got his sleeping place ready, but he had the first guard. The wilderness was dark. Beyond the campfire he saw the flicker of two green eyes close to the ground. He lit a stick and threw it. The eyes vanished.

36

As he walked on his lonely patrol, he paused at the sledge, stared reflectively at it, and finally dragged it to the firelight. One of the pegs was worn. He made a new one, and while the sledge was on its back, he gave the roller a push. It twirled in its pegs.

One side ran better than the other, he knew; it always had. It was the narrow end. The wider end scuffed and wore hard on the pegs. He pulled the roller free and held it up in the firelight; the pegs had worn little grooves into the roller.

It slipped easily back into place; the grooves helped. He gave it another twirl and watched. After a moment he brought an ax, intending to trim the wider end to the diameter of the smaller; he judged the cut, then hesitated, and put down the ax. The size itself wasn't the real problem, he knew, because he had seen rollers as thick as a man's body. The problem might be the difference in size.

He spun the roller across the ground; the large end traveled farther with each roll. If the ends were made even, the pole might roll evenly. He got a leather strip, wound it around the narrow end, and nailed it in place. Again he prodded the pole with his foot, watching closely, his dark eyes intent and squinting. The roller went straight.

He slipped it back, righted the sledge, and towed it a few paces. Seeing that the back dragged, he adjusted that, too, until the sledge finally rolled smoother than ever. He set the packs back on for the new day's march and straightened up. His knees and legs ached; he must have been at his work for a long time.

Smoke billowed up from the fire; the wind was changing. The moon slid up, yellow and clear over the plain. This was the first clear night of the journey; it could be a favorable sign. Ashna picked up his javelin and once more made a patrol around the sleeping camp.

4

The men were in good spirits the next day, for the sky was blue and clear. The onagers' hooves thudded on the rapidly drying soil.

Nagar still grumbled. "Summer comes. Now will Ninkilim, the god of rodents and vermin, send snakes and centipedes to plague us. Scorpions will crawl into our blankets. Flies will nip at our eyelids."

"This is a strange country," Mashkim said. "I have heard that there are mice which get up on their hind legs and run like little men."

Nagar told him that these were jerboas. "They eat

grain. They will climb into our packs."

Lugud's whoop came back. "Mountains!" he called. "The river divides. There is hilly ground, and a path to a great forest!"

"We are near the end of our journey," said Sint.

Mashkim said softly, "Look ahead! Men appear suddenly, as though they popped up from the ground."

Their way lay between two slopes, and on each were armed riders.

"Those are not Sumerians." Utul plucked at his curly beard.

Sint rode ahead. As his men waited nervously, he held up his hands to show that he came in peace.

"The strangers do not answer," Mashkim whispered.

Ashna saw Sint stop. There was a thunderous roar. Onagers shied. The Sumerians drew back.

"Stand still!" Lugud snapped. "That is only a drum. I have heard it before."

A rider galloped near, pounding two sticks at drums which hung from his onager's shoulders. Behind him came another rider, and from the brilliance of his blue and brown robes, Ashna guessed him to be a chieftain.

He spoke to Sint. Ashna did not understand, but his

41

older brother responded in the chieftain's own language.

Sint came back. "That is Kur, a chief. He says that his tribe owns this country. We must pay him to use the path."

Lugud growled and lifted his spear. Sint said, "Don't. We are surrounded."

THE FIRST WHEEL

"We had better pay." Nagar advised. "What does he want?"

"I would give him a spear in the heart," Lugud roared.

"Be quiet." Sint glanced back. "We must deal with him. We have to pass here again on our way downstream."

He talked with the chieftain. When he returned he said, "Kur wants a bag of barley for onager feed, and some metal spearheads."

"Barley is expensive now," Mashkim objected.

"Spearheads!" Lugud groaned. "We arm the enemy!"

"He wanted more at first," said Sint. "Unload the supplies." And to Lugud, Sint went on, "Kur is not an enemy — at least, not at this moment."

Sint handed over the supplies. The chief whirled around and was gone as quickly as he had come.

"Did you ask about onagers?" Ashna asked his oldest brother.

"That was the first thing I mentioned. They have none to sell at this time, but may when we come back this way."

The travelers entered the forest the next day. Before nightfall, they found what they sought: on the side of a steep hill, stumps of trees and a chute marked a logging place. It was on a small branch of the Euphrates.

43

"Make camp." Sint slid wearily down from his onager. "Bring the tablets, Ashna. You and I will climb the hill to find the person in charge of this place."

They started up. On a cliff above, men and oxen seemed as small as carvings in a temple frieze. Twice the brothers had to stop and move away as logs were pushed over the cliff. The logs bounced down the chute into the river.

At the top of the trail they stopped. "There are many men working up here," Sint said. Ashna looked about curiously.

A short man rode to them. He raised a whip. "You are Sumerians?" His language was broken, but Ashna understood.

"We are," Sint answered.

"What do you seek?" The man turned the onager so that it blocked Sint's view of the place.

"Timber. We would trade metal tools or feed grain. We want a hundred and twenty logs of good cedar; they should be of last year's cutting, so that they are seasoned and will float. We shall build rafts of some, and tow the rest."

The man studied Sint, and his sharp eyes did not miss

the boy. "You seek nothing else?" he asked suspiciously. "I am foreman here. You must account to me."

Sint considered. "After we have rafts, we must find copper ore. And we need onagers."

"We can spare no animals. You will have to find a mine elsewhere." The man edged his mount a little closer and fingered his whip. "I do not like Sumerians. You spy on us. And many of you are magicians.

"You will go back to your caravan," he continued to Sint, "and stay there. Send the boy back with some of the tools, that we may judge their value."

"Magicians!" Ashna began, but Sint interrupted. "We will do as you say. The boy will bring a metal saw and an axhead. These can be part of the trade. We will pay the rest after we get the cedar."

After further arrangements, the two went down the hill. "That was a strange meeting," Sint told his men. "They are not very friendly, and they suspect us of being magicians."

"They are probably sorcerers themselves," Mashkim grumbled. "Take Kur, for instance — he popped up out of the ground. I shall be glad to get home."

"Be careful." Sint handed the tools to Ashna. "That

45

foreman is suspicious. He did not want me to look across the hilltop."

"Sorcerers!" Mashkim muttered again.

On the hill, Ashna delivered the tools. The foreman checked them. As he did, Ashna saw ox teams labor across the stumpy ground. Woodchoppers made the forest echo with their blades. A whip cracked over slaves with a sledge.

"The tools are good," the foreman said. "Your cedar is over there. It is stacked crisscross to let the air dry it. I am sure that those two piles will be enough."

Ashna stared at where the man pointed. The cedar was indeed neatly stacked. "It is not quite enough. It lacks three."

"Lacks three!" the foreman exclaimed. "It does not." He slipped down from his onager and began to count the logs one by one. Ashna waited impatiently.

"A hundred and seventeen — " the foreman's eyes filled with suspicion. He lifted his whip. "It is said that you Sumerians are magicians. Now I see it for myself. Go!"

Ashna's face went white. "I used no magic. There are two stacks of logs, set evenly in rows of ten; they are six high except in one place. I multiplied ten by six, twice, and

subtracted — ”

"I do not know what you did, unless you called on a
Spirit of Numbers. That is magic, is it not?"

"It is arithmetic," Ashna said desperately, "which I
learned at the temple school."

Other loggers crowded around him. "Hear! The boy
admits it," one said. "He admits that he learns sorcery in
the Sumerian temple."

"I heard the whole argument," another declared. "No one can really count as fast as that."

Ashna drew back. "It is a simple thing — "

"Go away from us," the foreman shouted.

Ashna went down the stony trail. "Kill him now, before he puts an evil spell on us," he heard someone mutter.

"No, leave him alone," the foreman said. "We need the saws and axes."

At the camp, Ashna told his brothers. "The loggers were in a rage. I thought they would throw me over the cliff." He went on to explain.

They listened with understanding. "It is nothing new to us," Sint said. "Our mathematics is magic to them. So it is with astronomy, too, for we can foretell the seasons by the stars. Our engineers build canals like rivers springing from the ground; they plan temples which seem like mountains to the tribesmen. The desert nomads cross the plains in the autumn and see a mountain where none existed the year before. To them it is all magic."

"Whatever they think, we are in no danger until they get their tools," said Lugud thoughtfully. "But after that, we must be on guard."

"Why did they block Sint's view of the hilltop?" Mashkim asked. "Do they hide something — or someone?"

"Babbir!" Nagar blurted. "They may have him."

But Sint did not think so. "This is a remote region. Babbir left us far from here."

"They are hiding Sumerian slaves; I am sure of it."

Lugud growled. "We are too easy with everyone."

"No fighting if we can help it," said Sint quietly. "We must not risk a war for the sake of a few; those are the assembly's orders. Further, other Sumerians may need to trade here.

"Now the first logs come. Soon they will jam the river. We must set to work making boats of reeds, to tow the logs here; then we can begin our rafts."

Several round boats were quickly made, and eight long rafts slowly took shape along the riverside. The men worked from dawn to dark. They posted guards, for Lugud feared that the packs of shining new tools might be stolen.

When the rafts were finished, the rest of the cargo was stowed away and the onagers were led aboard and tied. The three brothers went up the hill with the packs of tools to pay for the logs.

The foreman and several others saw them come; they lined up their onagers so that the Sumerians could not see

49

past them. "Put the bags down," the foreman ordered. "We will count them before you go. Do not move."

A scribe turned the bags over. Ashna and his brothers waited while the tools were counted, one by one. When the scribe finally nodded to show that the total was as agreed, the foreman pointed with his whip. "You may go."

As the three started down, Lugud whispered, "Now, look out!"

Ashna glanced back, but he had to watch his footing on the rocky slope. He hurried to keep up. He heard a grating, snapping sound, hesitated, and once again glanced back. "Look out!" he yelled in fear. "A log!"

He flung himself at Sint, pushing him aside. They fell. Lugud sprang the other way. The log spun past.

As Ashna got up, he saw Lugud pull out a sling. No heavier weapons could be taken on the climb because of the packs. Lugud bounded back to within shooting distance.

A man peered over the edge of the cliff. Lugud lifted the sling. "Get back!" he bellowed. To Sint and Ashna he called, "Go on down. I'll give you a start."

Sint pulled at the boy's arm. They ran. Behind them there was silence. When they were at the bottom, they saw Lugud bolt from where he had stood. He plunged into deep

brush, running crookedly.

A second log tumbled off the cliff, away from the chute. Sint yelled a warning. But Lugud had gained a clump of trees. They saw him dodge behind a tree as a log crashed into it. The log stopped.

Lugud gave the log a kick with his foot and started it

down again. "Since you give these to us, we will take them," he roared. "Send some more!"

At this impudence the foreman shook his fist. Lugud bounded to the rafts. "Loosen the moorings," Sint shouted.

"Wait. Those logs. We will take them, just as I said." Lugud reached out with a pole. "Hold this one, Ashna, while I tie it. Now, the other — "

Sint called, "Hurry. The loggers leap up and down in their rage."

"They are no more dangerous now than dancing dolls." Lugud laughed. "Let them leap. We will go."

The rafts swung away. "Now the gods are with us, for there is a favorable wind and a fast current. We are safe." Ashna slumped down. He was still shaking from fright. But it did him good to see Lugud look back and laugh.

The Rafts Are Pursued

5

All that day they traveled. The first hot sun of summer poured down, and they made tent shelters on their rafts. At dusk they saw a village which they had passed to one side on their way upstream, when they had cut through the forest. Lugud and Sint went to trade. They brought back several apple and pomegranate saplings for the temple groves, and they had learned of a mine and a quarry downstream.

"We can reach them both tomorrow," Sint stated, "for at this mine we do not have to take rough ore; ingots are made which can be loaded quickly and which will take much less deck space. We can use the space for stone.

"We might reach the quarry, then, before night. If there is no delay, we can save several days."

The Sumerians were cheerful because they thought they would soon be home. They sang as they worked. Goatskin bags were blown full and fastened to the rafts which were to carry the copper and stone. Pegs were cut and rollers prepared for sledges.

From the village many people came to stare at the rafts. Some brought things to trade. Pigs squealed and

THE FIRST WHEEL

kicked as they were carried on by torchlight. Sheep stumbled about the decks with dogs barking at their hooves. On shore, a beggar came to play a reed pipe. The river echoed with noise.

Ashna was called from one place to another with his accounts as bags were emptied and refilled in barter. Nagar traded lengths of scarlet cloth for heaps of raw wool. Utul gave shiny copper jewelry for rough gem stones, carnelian and lapis lazuli.

In his raft shelter, Sint marked in the village, the mine, and the quarry on his clay maps. He called Ashna. "Make copies of these; other caravans will need them. Then total the several accounts. When we are sure that all the directions are correct, we will make copies of the maps for the temple records and have them baked and hardened to preserve the writing."

As the boy wrote, a stream of visitors met with the leader. Children from the village ran about, peered into the shelter, and chattered in their strange language.

It was late when Ashna finished. Lugud came to whisper something to Sint; then he went out to stand guard. Ashna blew out the little oil lamp and went to his sleeping place.

"Wait — I have something to tell you." Sint threw his cloak aside and straightened his own blanket. "Lugud saw the little man with the whip, the foreman of the loggers."

Ashna was startled. Sint said, "There were others of that mountain tribe with the foreman. I expect them to follow us. But we will get away from them. If you see them, be careful, but do not spread an alarm. We do not want a panic."

"I will say nothing," Ashna promised. "But why should they follow us so far?"

Sint was hesitant. "I am not sure. I do not want to make things seem worse than they are. Nothing may happen. Stay near the rafts. Do not go off alone."

Ashna stretched out under the blanket; he could hear the current slapping and rustling against the logs. Voices on shore faded away. As the moon came up, he could see Lugud pacing the deck, a bow and arrows across his broad shoulders.

The boy gazed at the moon: this was the god Enzu, flying across the sky. From up there, Enzu could see everything, and everyone. The moon god could see the city that was home. He could see Nin, Essna, and Ti'amat. The god could see Babbir, too. But where was Babbir? He had chosen to go in Ashna's place many days before. Ashna shivered. Whatever had happened to Babbir could have happened to him.

At daybreak the Sumerians were ready to go on. Sint went ashore for a last word with some of the villagers. When he returned, Ashna heard him tell Lugud that the mountain tribesmen had left during the night. "They may have given up the pursuit," Sint said.

They traveled on. At the mine they took on copper, and just as Sint had hoped, they reached the stone quarry before night.

The next day they made sledges and arranged to borrow oxen. Sint bargained for the size and shape of the stone he wanted; then blocks were lifted to the sledges and hauled to shore.

The sledges rasped with the friction of the rollers. They bumped over the rough ground; rollers fell out; pegs snapped. The days grew hot. The men were exhausted at night. But each day there was more to do.

Sint, Utul, and Ashna spent much of their time in cutting new rollers. "We use too many timbers," Sint said.

"Here is one that bears a charm," Utul told him. "It is the only one that goes smoothly. So straight does it go that the pegs wear neat little grooves."

"Try to find others like it." Sint took a moment to splash cold water from the river over his thick dark hair. He mopped at his head. "Or make them like it."

They tried a new log. But the men and oxen could not move it. In anger, Utul threw his ax down and jumped on it. Sint lay flat to peer under the sledge. "Try again."

"You might be crushed," Nagar warned.

"Move it," Sint insisted. Ashna goaded the oxen. Sint crawled around. "Halt!" He stood up and brushed at his clothes. "Something is still wrong."

Ashna said, "We could build up the narrower end with a few turns of leather stripping until it is the same thickness as the wide end. That worked with the onager sledge."

"A waste of leather," Utul objected.

"Try it." Sint was still patient. They did. This time the sledge rolled smoothly toward the raft. That night they finished loading. Sint was pleased. "Save those rollers. They make the best sledge I ever saw. We can copy them. I will draw a picture of them with the grooves and leather ends before they wear out."

A Fight in the Dark

6

Down the Euphrates the rafts floated, through hills green with new grass, past curves and turns, over rapids where the water churned deep and brown with mud. One day Sint called a halt very early. The men grumbled, for they wanted to hurry home. But Sint explained. "We are near the place of the high banks, where we could fall into an ambush. We will wait for darkness before going on."

Nagar asked, "What enemy is there to fear now?"

"The mountain tribesmen followed us to that village."

"They would not chase us this far!" Utul said. But his voice was doubtful.

"Oh, they would, if they thought they could take the rafts. The farther into the plains we go, the more valuable our cargo becomes. Had they attacked us earlier, they would have had to haul all these things south themselves to trade them. Now we have done all that work."

"If they capture the cargo and sell us as slaves, they will have a rich booty," Mashkim declared.

Nagar said, "We should fight."

"As yet there is no need to fight. We will try to avoid that. Now, tie up here. Lugud and Utul will scout toward the west; I will walk south with Nagar and search for a break in the embankment where the animals can be brought ashore to feed. Mashkim and Ashna will scout the east shore. Take a boat, and do not go far."

When Ashna and Mashkim landed, they tied the reed boat and set out across the plain. Except for a few thorn bushes, the land was barren. They climbed a rise.

"Tents!" Mashkim pointed. "That could be Kur's camp. Count the onagers — Sint will want to know how many there are."

"Thirty," Ashna said. "And there is one with drums tied to its shoulders."

"Then this is surely Kur's group." Mashkim suddenly pulled Ashna down behind a bush. "Someone comes."

A rider galloped by. They stayed motionless. "He did not see us." Mashkim sighed with relief. Abruptly he cried out in pain and brushed at his foot. "A scorpion."

Ashna stamped on the crawling thing. Mashkim hobbled away, his face pale. "Let's go back."

He leaned heavily on the boy's shoulder. At the river they stumbled down the bank, into the boat. Ashna pushed across as fast as he could.

On the raft, someone cut at the scorpion bite to draw the poison out. Mashkim howled in pain. "There are salves and medicines in my pack. Do something!"

"River mud is best at first," Lugud told him. He dabbed at the bite. "Later, some salve of grease and cedar oil could be put on. Now I will help you to the shelter."

Sint worried. "He will be lame for some days, and we need every man." Ashna heard what the other scouts had discovered: a group of mountain tribesmen were following but staying out of sight on the west shore. Down the river, Sint had located the crossing marked with a moon on his map. He saw many hoofprints there.

"There are tribesmen on one side, and Kur with his

bandits on the other," Nagar said gloomily. "Ahead there is a crossing where our rafts can get stuck. We cannot go back, because the current is too strong. And we cannot take our cargo over land, for it is too far for sledges."

The crewmen were silent. At last one suggested, "Pay Kur his toll, whatever he asks, and perhaps he will let us pass in safety near his side of the river."

"It is bad, either way," said Utul.

"Kur let us pass safely once before," Sint reminded them. "He was satisfied then. He may even be willing to trade this time. We will approach him."

They moored near the crossing. As the men tied the lines, Sint tested the depth of the water with a pole, searching for a clear place to slide the rafts through later on.

A voice hailed them. Ashna looked up. The high bank was crowded with armed men. Kur strode down, his robes billowing out, a dagger flashing at his belt. The Sumerians watched apprehensively as the bandit chief talked with Sint.

Sint translated. "Kur wants the same toll as before. And he says that he has some onagers and other valuable things. He would trade with us."

"Have him bring the onagers and valuables to the

river," Lugud suggested. "We will unpack some barley and spearheads."

Mashkim was elated. "We worried for nothing!"

Kur rode away. He soon returned and shouted to Sint.

"We are to go up there," the Sumerian leader explained. "Lugud, Utul, Ashna, bring the supplies and account tablets."

At the top of the embankment they stopped in surprise. "Babbir!" Lugud hissed. "They have him!"

"Say nothing," Sint warned. "He is guarded." He stepped forward to talk with Kur.

The chieftain explained that when Babbir had tried to catch up with the caravan, he had been taken prisoner because he had nothing to offer as a toll. He had been cared for these many, many days, and had eaten large amounts of food which now must be paid for —

"Kidnappers!" Lugud growled. "Robbers, black-mailers!"

"Kur thinks it is quite reasonable." Sint's lips drew into a thin line. His black eyes flashed. "Keep your temper. We must get Babbir back unharmed."

The tall man was now for sale, Kur continued, and so

were the two splendid onagers over there.

Sint stared "Splendid onagers! The mare is good. But the other is just a colt, a helpless foal. Something is the matter with it: it does not stand up."

Ashna bent over the colt. "This little one has a bad leg. It has been injured somehow."

"The foal is of no use to us," Sint said to Kur.

Kur smiled broadly. The rich Sumerians must take all or nothing. The price would be the first four of the eight rafts.

"We will hold a council," Sint said calmly. "We will tell you before dark." He motioned to the other Sumerians to return with him to the rafts.

"That is half of everything!" Lugud roared in anger when he heard the price. "We would not dare to face the assembly with but half our cargo."

Sint's face was lined with worry. "Would you dare to tell the assembly that you would not save Babbir?"

The men were bewildered. No answer seemed right. Finally Utul said, "Let us do whatever Sint suggests."

"We may have to fight," the leader said grimly. "And Mashkim is lame."

"I can shoot arrows from here." The stout man sat up awkwardly.

"Even with you, and counting the boy, they out-number us," Nagar asserted.

They talked of a surprise attack to free Babbir. But someone pointed out that this would leave the rafts open to assault by the mountain men on the other shore.

"I wish that they would come right now," Ashna began to say. He flushed when everyone stared. "Kur would surely demand a toll of them, too. If there were a way to set our enemies upon each other, we might snatch Babbir away."

"That is madness!" Nagar snarled. "You are only a boy. Keep still!"

But Lugud's eyes widened with the thought. "It might be done! If I went upstream and lured the tribesmen to this place just at dark, they might attack Kur."

"Oh, let us flee now," said Utul in a shaky voice.

"Kur would ride along the high bank and cut us down like nesting birds," Lugud retorted. "At this very moment we are safe only because he thinks we are going to surrender to him."

"True," Utul admitted, and the others agreed.

"We will do as Ashna suggested," said Sint. "It might work. But even if it does not, I feel that we must try to rescue Babbir."

The Sumerians made their plans. At dusk, Sint went to see Kur and asked for more time to consider. Kur grumbled, but finally agreed.

At the same time, Lugud rode up the opposite bank with Nagar, talking loudly about gathering a few snails and worms for fish bait, and arguing about whether Tigris or Euphrates salmon were the best. One of Kur's patrols saw them, as the Sumerians expected they would, but the nomads made no move to follow.

On the rafts the men waited restlessly. The darkness grew thicker. After what seemed an endless time, they heard hooves pounding along the river bank. Lugud and Nagar splashed into the shallows. As they hurried their onagers aboard, Lugud flashed a warning glance at Sint. Sint nodded in understanding.

A torch flared on Kur's side, and an angry voice demanded to know if anyone passed without paying a toll.

"My brother returns," Sint called.

"Tell them I brought some excellent bait," Lugud whispered. "Oh, you should have seen the tribesmen. We pretended to blunder into their camp. I knocked a guard down with a stone from my sling." He grunted in satisfaction. "It was like throwing a stone into a hive of bees."

"Listen!" Sint cautioned Lugud to silence.

"I hear the tribesmen," said Nagar.

"Tell Kur's men to light another torch," Lugud said softly. "Say that I lost something and cannot see."

"Pick up your spears," said Sint grimly. There was a

thunder of hooves on the far bank. A light glowed. Then in Kur's camp a drum rolled fiercely.

"Now they will collide in the dark," Nagar said in awe.

Sint spoke quickly to Lugud. "We will try to get Babbir now. Get ashore — this way."

No one was prepared for what happened next. A figure hurtled through the gloom and slammed against the deck. Ashna cried out and dodged to one side. Lugud whirled and threw himself at the figure.

"Let go — it is I, Babbir." Lugud stepped back in astonishment. As Babbir struggled to his feet, another dark shape leaped to the raft. It stumbled in front of the raft shelter.

"Babbir's guard!" Sint yelled.

Mashkim's bow lashed out like a club. Lugud hauled the guard to the edge of the raft and hurled him overboard. "He fell on my wounded ankle," Mashkim said angrily.

Then everyone turned to watch fearfully as a line of shadowy riders hit the water and plunged across toward the bright torches on Kur's side.

"The tribesmen," Ashna said. "They may see us here."

"We must be still," whispered Sint. "Now they rush at each other." The terrible sound of battle rose on the river bank. Babbir clutched at Sint's shoulder. "Kur will kill me if he catches me. Let us go, anywhere."

"Wait." A last rider was crossing; abruptly he reined in. "He sees us," someone said hoarsely.

Lugud hurled his javelin. The rider fell. "Now!" Sint exclaimed. He sent a command to the other rafts. The rafts lurched out into the river. Ashna stared back. "They are throwing their torches into the water!"

The darkness thickened. Lugud listened to the battle sounds with an expert ear. "They both think they fight us," he said. "Each is taken aback at the strength of the other."

The sounds behind them rapidly grew faint. "The tribesmen flee one way and Kur the other. Both have had enough." Lugud chuckled.

"I dare not go too far," Sint said after a while. "We are beyond those high banks. There may be other shallows ahead. I cannot see clearly. We could run aground."

"We are safe now," Lugud assured him. "Pull over to one side until daybreak. Tomorrow we can get to Hit."

When the rafts were moored, Babbir told his story.

70

Kur had put him under guard on the river bank, near the onager and her colt. When the attack started, his guard had turned away for an instant, and Babbir had bolted.

"What of the mare?" Lugud asked.

Babbir tried to recall. "I think she was tied to a stake. She is probably still there."

Sint said, "I know what you are thinking, Lugud, but that is a long way back. The onager is not worth the risk."

"There may be others, those whose riders have fallen," Lugud protested.

But Sint shook his head. As the night wore on, the old sounds of the wilderness returned. A hyena prowled

near, then scuttled away as it scented the rafts. A night-bird chirped. Far away, a wolf howled.

"No one moves back there," Lugud spoke again to Sint. "The place is deserted save for wild animals. The onager would be valuable. We have not been able to buy a single one, and we are missing the one Kur took from Babbir."

When Sint did not reply, Lugud persisted. "By day-break, wolves or lions will have killed it. If it is tied, it cannot run or defend itself."

"If you go, you go alone," Nagar said. "I have had enough excitement for this night."

"I would go!" Ashna said quickly.

Sint finally gave his permission. The boy picked up his weapons and followed Lugud.

"Do you know why the boy wanted to go?" Babbir said after a while. "That foal. He saw it when you bargained with Kur. He wants the foal for himself."

Sint was startled. "I should have guessed." He glared angrily into the darkness. "I dare not make a noise to call them back.

"The colt will be of no use to him; it has a bad leg. Bringing it to trade was one of Kur's tricks."

"He wants an onager of his own," Mashkim said. "He has wanted one for a long time."

The leader paced back and forth. "How could they get it back here? It is a long way. They should seize the mare and run off with her. They should not stay in that place a moment longer than they have to."

Ashna Finds a Colt

7

Near the battlefield, Lugud and Ashna stopped to listen. A wolf howled. The sound was close. Lugud took this as a sign. "None of the men are near — at least, not now."

Ashna followed his bulky shape. "Over there," Lugud whispered. The mare shied away.

"Here — quiet — " Lugud seized its rope and yanked up the stake. "Ashna, get on its back — I'll lead."

"The foal," the boy said. "I want to take it."

"But it is worthless," Lugud exclaimed. "Come, Ashna!"

The boy still hesitated. "If we leave it here, the wild animals will kill it." He kneeled over the small, warm body; it trembled as he touched it. "We could make drag poles of our spears and get it back that way."

"You do not understand," Lugud answered. "It may never be strong. Leave it here. We must get back."

Ashna turned away. Tears smarted in his eyes. Dimly he saw Lugud tug at the mare's head.

The mare balked. "Move, stubborn one." Lugud swung a spear at her flank. "Move along, or you will be food for the wolves."

Ashna tried to help, but the mare reared and kicked. He stepped aside. "She will not go without her foal."

"She must." Lugud hit her again. Finally he gave up. "You are right, Ashna. Make a dragger of the spears. We'll tie the foal to the spears with the rope from the stake."

This time the mare obeyed. Ashna was jubilant.

In the haze of dawn, the rafts slid away from their mooring place. The sun rose red and hot. The water was smooth, and on both sides the land was still and deserted.

Ashna jumped from raft to raft, to where the onagers

were tied. A crewman shouted at him, "You travel farther, back and forth, than we will go today!"

Babbir was amused. "That colt will not run away. Indeed, it will never run!"

"Leave the boy alone." Mashkim hopped about, regaining the use of his foot. "Some of us might not be here now had not the boy suggested a way out of that ambush."

It was true, the men knew. They said no more about the colt, although Sint and Lugud watched the boy with something like despair.

Ashna tried to wrap the colt's leg with a cloth. He brought water and barley feed. Later, Mashkim hobbled back, carrying a jar of pasty ointment. "Try this. They used it on my foot. It might help."

"The colt's leg is not as swollen as it was last night, is it?"

"I did not see it then," Mashkim said. "But a leg injury to an onager is a most serious one."

"I know that," Ashna said. "But I will try to save the colt. It is very good-looking, is it not? See how it moves its long ears when I scratch its head."

Mashkim scratched his own head. "A very handsome beast. Ashna, I am grateful to you for helping me when

I was bitten. Take the ointment." He was going to add his doubt about the hope of saving the onager, but Ashna was not listening. He was using the medicine and making another bandage.

At Hit the rafts stopped for the asphalt, a tarry substance that would be used for glue, for patching seams in buildings, and for waterproofing. Sides were built up on one raft to increase its load.

Utul asked for leave to visit his relatives in the city. When he returned, he said to Sint, "My people say that a chief of a nomad group came through here. From the description, he could be Kur."

"He would be far from his country," said Sint.

"The chief asked about a string of rafts and their destination. He knew some of the crew: a tall, thin man; a boy with dark hair, twelve or thirteen years old; a broad-shouldered warrior with a roaring voice."

"Babbir, Ashna, and Lugud," said Sint.

"When the chief found that we were here at Hit, he left in great haste, riding to the south."

When Sint told the crewmen, someone said, "Kur wants revenge."

"He cannot stop us now," Lugud declared. "The

plains are too flat for ambush. The Euphrates is wide; we can float home in safety."

The men were alert, nevertheless. As they left Hit, they watched both shores. They saw no one. At last the black shape of the temple loomed up in the distance. The rafts swung into the canal; they needed no towing, for the current went east. They sped homeward.

A crowd waited for them. Ashna jumped ashore and ran to embrace his mother and to talk excitedly with Ti'amat and Essna. Then there was the great activity of unloading the cargoes.

Ashna asked his father to look at the onager colt. Essna suddenly frowned. "I know that you have it. I do not care to see it now."

Unhappy at his father's brusque tone, Ashna returned for the colt. Some crewmen had succeeded in getting the balky mare to shore, and now the colt was alone. Ashna stared at it.

"I am in trouble again, I think," the boy muttered to the colt, "and I would guess that you are, also." He saw Mashkim with a sledge and hailed him for a place for the colt.

"I have room," the stout man said.

"Ashna!" It was Sint's voice. The two older brothers and Essna were together, not far away.

Mashkim and a crewman were already picking up the colt. "I'll have it put in your stable," Mashkim promised. "Go to your brothers. I think you will hear some news that will not please you. I am sorry."

Worry hit Ashna with the sharpness of an arrow. He joined his brothers.

Sint said, "Father has a report from the assembly. We called you to hear it with us."

"Kur has been here," their father said. "He and several of his lieutenants came and spoke to the assembly. He left before you came."

Essna turned to Sint. "Kur claimed that your crew tricked him into a battle with some strangers from the mountains, that you passed his camp without a toll, that you refused to trade, and that you stole two of his onagers. He demands payment for all his losses."

Essna seemed older than Ashna remembered. He ran his fingers through his gray hair. "I did not believe Kur. But he is a powerful chief; you saw only one of his many groups. The assembly is anxious to come to friendly terms with him because our caravans pass through his country."

"Kur spoke but half the truth," Lugud said angrily. "The assembly should not judge until they hear us."

"I will speak for you," said Essna. "But our officials feel that some payments will be necessary, whatever the truth."

"Kur wanted half the rafts!" Sint burst out. "We cannot give in to him. Like Lugud, I'd rather fight. He held Babbir for ransom for lack of a toll — "

"That is tribal custom," Essna said evenly. "But go on."

After Sint explained, Essna admitted, "I might have done much the same if I had been in command.

"But leaving the onagers on the shore seems like a trick," Essna continued. "Kur may have left them there intentionally, hoping that you would return for them. Now he has told the assembly that you stole the animals from him."

"Kur had Babbir's onager — and the colt is worthless," Lugud exclaimed.

Essna smiled grimly. "The colt was not so worthless that you would leave it. Do you see now the kind of tale Kur had for the city officials? Even those who doubted Kur will see that Ashna has the colt."

"What will happen?" Ashna asked.

"That is for the assembly to decide. Kur may be paid a toll. I do not know about the mare."

"And the colt?"

"You are too concerned about a useless animal," Essna snapped. "You try to save it against everyone's advice."

Ashna said, "But it was so helpless there in the desert — wolves would have got it. And the mare balked when we tried to take her without it."

"You show too much pity," Essna said coldly. "I remember how you pitied that young slave. You are too gentle."

"Ashna does not lack for personal courage," said Lugud.

"He must face the pain or death of others, or of a mere animal, without flinching. He is my son. He must be more manly."

Ashna walked away. He felt as though he had been whipped. In the house which he had not seen for so long, Ti'amat and Nin were preparing another feast. But he turned away and went to the stable.

The colt lay quietly on a bed of straw. He stroked its

head and examined the leg. "It is not as swollen now. Here, try to stand up."

He pulled at the animal's shoulders. But it tottered and slumped down.

Ti'amat came in. "So this is the little onager that I heard about. Let me see its leg. What have you done to heal it?"

When Ashna told her, she said, "You have tried nearly everything except hot water and salt."

"We have not had hot water since we left."

"I will get some." Ti'amat brought water and bathed the colt's leg. When she put the salt on, the animal struggled.

Ti'amat jumped away. "The salt burns. But he kicked that leg well enough then; here, hold him down."

She put on more salt. The colt squealed and brayed. Then in a flash it was standing in a corner, quivering, its head tossing.

"Oh, he walked!" Ashna said exultantly. "Ti'amat, you did it!"

"He still must have a bandage. Hold him."

Ti'amat's nimble fingers fastened the cloth. "Now you may let him go." She stood back to appraise her work.

"It is good. Do you have a name for him?"

"Not yet," said Ashna.

"Try a name that will remind you of where you found him."

Ashna's dark eyes clouded over. "I will never need to be reminded of that."

"You found him in the night, didn't you? Call him that."

Ashna looked gratefully at Ti'amat. "You have helped him. Call him anything you like."

"Night!" Ti'amat said briskly. She pointed at the trembling colt. It laid back its ears and brayed.

Ashna laughed for the first time that day. "Night it is, then!"

A Faster Sledge for Night

8

The assembly called the crewmen to report on the journey. Ashna, because of his youth, was the only one not asked.

"I wonder what will happen," he said to his mother. "The assembly could make me give Night back to Kur."

"You will have to do whatever they say," Nin answered. "However, Sint and Lugud will speak for you."

"Will Essna? He is an official. He could say something." Ashna wandered over to the shrine. The clay god seemed to stare into space; it told him nothing.

"Essna thinks I am too gentle," Ashna went on.

"This is a harsh world, and these are harsh times."

"But Essna criticizes me in front of the others."

"If he did not care, he would not criticize," Nin said. "He is an official and strict with everyone because he knows it is best. Sometimes he is more strict with his own sons, because he cares even more. He would have you grow to be like Sint and Lugud."

"I don't think I will ever be like them."

Nin smiled. "You will."

When his brothers returned, Ashna asked what had happened.

"Some were pleased with the reports, others were not," Sint told him. "Kur will be sent his tolls. And when the barley is in, some will be given to him for the injuries his group suffered. Babbir will get the mare in exchange for his own onager."

"But the colt!"

"If it is kept, it must be paid for," said Lugud. "But you couldn't pay; your earnings from the trip are not enough. And Essna says it is not worth a handful of feed."

"I will keep Night somehow." Ashna was determined. "I do not understand why we give Kur all he asks."

Lugud cut in. "Nor do I!"

"No one wanted the colt. It was left to die." Ashna could have said more, but it was not for a boy to find fault with the assembly.

Ti'amat said, "Night took his first steps today. His leg is not so swollen."

They went to see Night. Sint said, "I could pay some of the cost of the colt from my earnings."

Lugud was looking at Ashna instead of the colt. "I could, too, if Essna would permit it."

It was a quiet family that gathered that evening, despite the fact that they were together for the first time in more than a month. While Nin served another feast, Ashna waited for one of his brothers to speak. Essna said very little.

"We have a request," Sint said at last. "Ashna wants to give up his pay for the colt. Lugud and I are pleased with his work on the trip. He made no mistakes in the accounts; he complained less than the others; and most important of all, we may owe our lives to him, for he first saw the log that was meant to kill us. He gave the warning."

Essna listened intently as Sint went on. "Ashna's pay

is not enough for the colt. Lugud and I are willing to meet the rest of the cost."

"But the colt may not live. Even if it does, it may always have a weak leg. It could carry no pack or rider," Essna said. "The cost of its feed may be wasted."

"The colt will live," said Ti'amat quickly. "I think its leg will heal."

Ashna held his breath. Essna sighed. "Let the boy have it, then."

Ashna's heart seemed to turn over. Essna spoke on. "During the summer, Lugud and Sint will show Ashna more about hunting and fighting. Teach him to throw a spear from a running onager, and to use a sling. These are manly things."

Ashna saw that his father still thought of him as too gentle. But he was elated at keeping the colt, and the idea of hunting with his brothers pleased him greatly.

"It is settled." Sint thanked Essna, and added, "Ashna may some day be more than a hunter. He is good at arithmetic, and should continue at the temple school. He is so quick with numbers that the loggers thought he was a magician."

"He might be a designer some day." Lugud grinned.

"He might plan a canal or a temple." These were interesting ideas, Ashna admitted. But his head was full of more interesting ones — what to do next with Night, for example.

As the assembly directed, Kur was paid. Traffic to and from the city went on again. There was no lack of crewmen now, because the planting season was over, and the blazing summer heat caused most of the work in the city to stop.

Lugud and Sint were free to hunt in the plains and eastern hills. They ranged far in pursuit of gazelle, stag, and antelope, and with them Ashna learned many of the skills of a hunter and warrior. Ashna became thirteen years old that summer. He had grown a good deal taller, and Sint said he was sunburned as brown as one of Kur's nomads.

There were many days when Ashna spent time with the colt, too. He trained it and watched it grow, month by month. On Mashkim's advice, he let Night graze in the marshes. "It is good for his hooves and legs," the stout man said.

As Night trotted and ran through the marsh, Ashna gathered reeds for weaving and plaiting baskets, or fished in the canal. He taught Night to come when he whistled, to stand still, to carry small packs, and to drag poles. But one day Night slipped in the soft ground. When he got up, he seemed to have sprained his leg.

"It is the same leg!" the boy exclaimed. "Oh, Night, you will never be well."

He led Night home. When Ti'amat saw the colt, she said, "It does not seem to be a bad injury."

Ashna was afraid that she was wrong. "We must bandage him again."

Ti'amat bound the colt's leg. "He lies down of his own accord," she observed. "This time, keep him off that leg until it is thoroughly healed, so that he does not make a habit of that limp."

They kept a close watch on Night. Ashna made a bit and bridle and a small yoke for him. "When we do let you up, we will make you work," he muttered to the colt. "You will learn. You will be strong."

In due time Ashna let the colt walk to the marsh again. Ti'amat followed, watching closely. "He has not limped once! He may be cured," she said.

"I hope you are right," said Ashna. But he let most of the summer go by before resuming the colt's training.

Then he tried Night with a small sledge.

The sledge dragged noisily; Night's long ears went back in fright. He kicked the sledge to pieces.

Ashna was alarmed. "Don't do that. You will hurt your leg again — stubborn little beast!"

The boy picked up the pieces and began a better sledge. After a few moments he stopped and went to find Sint.

"You drew a picture of the good rollers we had at the stone quarry. Let me see it," he said.

Sint brought the tablet to the stable. "You have the idea. Your sledge is like the picture."

"It isn't good enough." Ashna spun a roller. "The roller falls out — but it doesn't when the sledge is upside down."

"It can't; the body and the pegs hold it."

"I could fasten a leather thong here, from peg to peg, along the groove. It would hold the roller up. The leather would not rub the ground, either, because it would be slid into the groove."

Sint understood. He helped to fasten the leather. When they were finished, they tried the sledge. It rattled, but it worked fairly well.

Night lifted his head at the sound and brayed loudly.

"The colt doesn't like it," Ashna said anxiously.

Sint laughed. "He must. It is a good sledge. I am going to mark that thong on the tablet."

Ashna studied the rough drawing. "Those were big rollers."

"They were for oxen, not onagers," Sint reminded him.

"They covered more ground with each turn. Mine turn four or five times before going so far."

Sint said, "That is true. Large logs turn less, but go farther."

"I could get a good roll from these small logs if I built up the ends. Night could haul them easily."

"You persist so!" Sint laughed. "Leather is scarce. Find some broken harness or reins; they will do for what you want."

Ashna hunted through the stable. When he had found all the leather he could, he bound the ends of the rollers with several thick layers.

Sint had gone long before Ashna finished, and Nin was calling impatiently for him to come to the evening meal. But he was pleased with the sledge. One push of

his foot sent it crawling in a straight line across the stable.

When he finally went into the house, he said to Sint, "It works now. I built the ends up to get a roll like a thicker log without the weight and rub. Now when I push the sledge, it scuttles along as if it were alive."

Sint's dark eyes narrowed in imagining. "It would, if

93

you built up the ends enough."

"The food is getting cold," Nin complained.

"All that time and work for a colt of doubtful value," said Essna impatiently.

"His sledge is worth copying," Sint replied. "Anything that we can do to improve the everlasting hauling and carrying will be of benefit to us." He found the tablet with the sketch and showed it to Essna. "This is what we developed."

Essna bent over the tablet. "It is a simple thing. Now, why didn't anyone think of that before! What is this mark?"

Lugud got up to see, too. Nin threw up her hands. "Come, Ti'amat," she said, "you and I will eat alone. Their thoughts are on sledges and transport, and they are as far from us as the north country."

94

The First Wheel

9

When the meal was over, the men came to see the sledge. "It is clever," Essna admitted. "A small log rolls like a large one, with very little drag."

"Exactly," exclaimed Sint. "Ashna has obtained the wide sweep of a large roller, with the lesser weight of the small log."

Lugud crouched down. "This is off the ground in the center. Only the ends touch — the center rolls free." He tapped impatiently at Sint's leg. "Get down here. See this."

"I saw it before. The drag is less because the part

that rubs the sledge is much narrower."

Lugud saw the strip which went from peg to peg. "And this keeps the roller from falling out. It doesn't touch the ground, either, because Ashna has it in a groove."

"It has one fault," Essna said. "That is the cost of leather."

"But it would save labor," answered Sint. "We have all seen sledges so clumsy that they needed four oxen, when with good rollers, two oxen could have made them move."

Lugud said, "With a sledge like this, one ox could haul a very heavy burden."

"You do not know that for a certainty," Essna reminded him. "Sint can make a full-sized sledge from Ashna's model. If it works as well as you think, I'll show it to the assembly."

It was several days before Sint could begin the sledge, because he was called to plan the staging for a temple wall. Ashna's lessons began again, and he found less time for the colt.

When Sint finally started, he set Ashna's sledge near, to copy it. Sint had everything he needed: tools, nails, logs, and long lengths of leather. The shiny tools fascinated Ashna, and he liked the scent of fresh-cut wood.

"The strips are next," Sint said. He tacked an end. "It will take a lot of leather," he observed. "I can see what Essna meant about the expense."

"Could something else be used?" asked Ashna.

"It must wind around and be tough, yet pliable."

"Could we cut off the end of a large log and fasten it to a smaller one?"

Sint looked thoughtfully at the end of a log. "The whole end?"

"This much." Ashna pointed.

Sint shook his head. "You would have nails running parallel to the grain or lines of the wood. That is called end-nailing, and any carpenter would tell you that end-nails do not hold. Further, wood on its end-grain is weak; it splits."

"May I use the saw?" When Sint said that he could, Ashna began a long deep cut. Sint finished the strip and took the saw from Ashna.

"I'll finish this for you," said Sint. The disc of wood soon fell off.

Ashna propped it against Night's small sledge. He

lifted a roller, held it to the disc to make a mark, and set it down.

"Now what?" Sint asked. Ashna was searching amongst the tools.

"I want to cut a hole through the disc and slip it onto the roller."

Sint said, "I will make that cut for you, too." As he did it, he commented, "You are trying to improve the

THE FIRST WHEEL

roller. But you must consider the time it takes. I wouldn't want to do this very often."

"I can do the other discs," Ashna said.

"You will have to. I have other work to do." Sint handed him the tools. "Be careful. These are sharp."

Ashna carried the heavy disc to the small sledge and fitted it in place. At once he saw that it would not stay. He would have to put a peg through the roller.

It took him the rest of the day to make a second disc and to bore holes in the end of the roller for pegs. When he was finished, both discs turned with the small log or axle. The roller then turned quite well. Ashna was not sure that the sledge would be a better one, but he felt that it might; later he would add discs to the back roller. He stretched his fingers wearily, and saw a blister on his palm from gripping the saw and borer.

Ashna picked up Sint's tools and brought them into the house. The thought that he and Sint had invented the first wheel never occurred to him; it was just a better roller. What it would do remained to be seen.

The harvest season was welcomed with a great ceremony at the temple. The Sumerians offered thanks to their

moon god and to Ninhursaga, the goddess of soil, and
Ninsar, goddess of plants. Slaves and citizens alike went
to the fields to bring in the grain.

Ashna was as busy as the rest, and his sledge lay un-
finished. Lugud and Sint were sent with a caravan to Hit
to get asphalt for waterproofing the temple granaries.

As time went on, Night grew larger and stronger. He
had no trace of a limp now. He learned to respond to
Ashna's whistles, and to stay at his heels like a good dog.
From bearing small packs to carrying a rider would be but
a small step, the boy hoped, but Lugud had advised him to
wait until spring.

Ashna finally cut the other discs for the sledge. He
evened them up with leather and pegged the axles in place.
The sledge finished, he fastened a harness and with both
hands gave the sledge the usual hard pull.

It nearly knocked him over. Startled, he stepped
aside, then cautiously prodded it with his foot. The cart
— for that is what it was — veered across the stable and
slammed into the wall.

Ashna yelled in surprise. Unbelievingly he stared at
the cart, then ran from the stable.

As he came into the house, Ti'amat asked, "What is

the matter with you?"

He pulled her by the arm. "I will show you. Come." She followed him to the stable.

"Now watch." He pulled the cart.

Ti'amat gasped. "Let go of it. It will roll upon us."

"Get on. I think I can haul you around — "

"Not on that." Ti'amat stepped back. "It gives me chills to watch it. What makes it go like that?"

"I'll get on. You pull." Ashna leaped up. "Go on, Ti'amat, pull!"

Just as Ashna had done, she gave much too hard a pull. The cart clattered ominously toward her. She shrieked and fled into the house.

Ashna fitted a small yoke to Night. "You could haul this, and me also. But I will fasten a shaft, a light pole, from the frame to your yoke so that the fast-roller does not chase you around as it did me. I don't want it to bump into your legs. Hold still — "

He led the colt outside, sat on the front of the cart, and flapped the reins. Night turned and stared at him.

"What kind of thing is that?" Ashna heard his mother ask. She and Ti'amat were watching.

"It is a fast-roller. Ti'amat, lead Night."

"I'll do that, but do not ask me to ride up there."
Ti'amat led Night back and forth. When the colt seemed
used to the idea, Ashna got him going without Ti'amat.

Night trotted forward briskly. The cart lumbered
along the road. The discs raised a cloud of dust.

"Go on," Ashna yelled. Night trotted faster. Al-

THE FIRST WHEEL

though the rollers were off the ground, they still rubbed the pegs and frame in places, and from this steady friction there came a dull moan. As the cart went faster, the moan rose to a shriek. Night's ears went back. He galloped.

"Stop!" Ashna saw people dodging. He yanked the reins. "Stop!" Quivering, the onager obeyed. Ashna walked him back. Everyone was looking; most were as frightened as Night had been.

Later Essna saw the cart, and he too was amazed at its ease of movement. At Ashna's insistence, he yoked a pair of oxen to it and piled on several sacks of feed.

"That is as much as I would expect the oxen to haul," Essna said. "Start them."

The cart rolled easily. "Put more on!" said Ashna eagerly. Essna did. The cart creaked and groaned, but it moved.

"Enough," Essna said. "The frame is sagging. We do not want to break it. Let's try these rollers on Sint's heavy sledge."

When the axles and discs were transferred, the boy and his father increased the burden even more. Ashna led the oxen forward.

"It moves!" Essna said in awe. "Why, that is a load that would strain four oxen. Sint and Lugud were right. This could save the city a tremendous amount of labor.

"Two hundred oxen could do the work of four hundred. Our transport could be doubled. Many oxen could be freed for plowing. It is an ingenious device. You have done well, Ashna!"

The boy flushed under his praise. Essna added, "I will show it to the assembly."

"There is something you should know," Ashna said. "I had it on the road. As the discs spun faster and faster, they made a screeching sound. It is frightening. Everyone ran away."

"I remember that Ti'amat was frightened."

"We could unload the frame, take off the discs and rollers, and put the whole thing together when we reach the temple."

Essna agreed to this. The next day they harnessed the oxen to the sledge and pulled it to the temple grounds. The officials were curious as Essna demonstrated with loads of barley and emmer. When a burden was reached that the oxen could not move on rollers, he had a group of slaves unload the sledge and turn it over. He and Ashna put the wheeled axles in place.

The sledge was now a heavy cart. The slaves put the load back on. Essna called for still more bags. At this the officials shook their heads doubtfully.

"It is a very good sledge," one man called, "but you should not injure the oxen just to impress us."

Essna did not reply. He beckoned to Ashna; the two stepped up on the front of the cart.

"Take the reins," said Essna.

The boy yelled, "Yo! Move!" The cart creaked.

Ashna yelled again. From the axles there came an ominous whine. The oxen lumbered ahead. The whine became a squeal, louder and louder.

The slaves cried out and ran. As the cart screeched across the yard, the officials clapped their hands over their ears and fled in every direction.

Suddenly there was a crack, and the cart tipped heavily to one side. Startled, Ashna hauled at the reins, then lost his balance and had to jump. Essna leaped from the other side and lunged for the bridle. He halted the team.

Ashna straightened up. "The disc!" he said in dismay. "It is broken!"

"Never mind that — are you all right?"

When Ashna said that he was, Essna glanced around. The yard was still empty. "Pick up the pieces of the disc and the bags which fell off. We will unload the fast-sledge."

Some minutes went by before the men ventured back into the yard.

"It is the Voice of Enlil, god of thunder and force," a white-faced official told Essna.

"You have a living beast made of wood," another

bleated. "A monster, a crawling, scuttling thing from the underworld."

Another cried, "Magic! It is not natural for two oxen to run with the load of four!" The council became an uproar. The frightened slaves would not approach the cart to finish the unloading.

"Take the fast-roller home," said Essna quietly. When the boy started, the axle ploughed into the ground and another disc split apart. The oxen dragged the broken cart as it was. Chagrined, the boy glanced back. But the officials were not looking. They were circling Essna and talking loudly.

Lugud Is Captured

10

"The fast-roller broke," Ashna said unhappily to Nin.

"Sint will help you repair it," she replied.

"The idea was not good. It may not be worth the time." He waited uneasily for Essna.

When Essna returned, he said, "The assembly says that your fast-roller should be in the temple. There the carpenters will try to make another like it. But some men are afraid it cannot be copied, because it is magical."

"Magical!" exclaimed Ashna. "It was too much hard

work to be magic. Those discs are hard to cut. I blistered my hands. And the fast-roller is for Night."

"I am sorry you have to give it up," Essna said, "but you should be honored at the interest the assembly has — "

"But those carpenters can easily make all the discs they need. They have temple tools and enough wood."

Essna said, "Do not be so stubborn. When it is seen that your roller is not magic, it may be returned."

Ashna watched unhappily as Essna brought the cart to the temple grounds and left it there. But that same day some news came which made the cart and Night seem unimportant.

Sint and Babbir returned in desperate haste. Their onagers were streaked with sweat and desert dust. Babbir's left arm was bleeding from an arrow wound.

"We were attacked. The whole caravan is gone," Babbir said hoarsely. "It was Kur."

Sint leaned wearily against his onager. "Lugud, Mashkim, all the rest were captured. We escaped. We must gather a force and go after them."

Essna's face went gray. "The assembly will not fight. Our men are lost!"

"We must fight." Sint's old calmness was gone. "We lost thirty men — and I know that at least three were slain."

"Put Babbir between us. Get him inside," said Essna.

They heard the rest. Nin and Ti'amat listened in horror. Kur had attacked late at night, overpowering a sentinel and falling upon the travelers as they slept.

"Kur must have a hundred tribesmen with him," Sint said. "It was a hopeless fight. Babbir and I were near the onagers, or we would not have escaped. We had no time to reach for our weapons before they were upon us. We mounted and fled."

The council met immediately, but few men wanted a war. One said, "Even supposing we should defeat the tribesmen — and they can muster more warriors than we — we might not get our men back. Kur might sell them to us, but he would have them killed before he would let us recapture them."

"Kur has nothing to lose in a war," another pointed out. "He carries only a few tents and lives off the land or by preying upon travelers. But we have our city to lose!"

Essna said, "I do not speak only because my son Lugud is among the captives. There are many others, and still more Sumerians are being held as slaves in the north-land. We cannot let this go on. We should send a mighty force."

"We should make a firm stand now!" Sint said. "Not only Kur, but all people, would respect us for it."

Some men agreed, but Essna and Sint were overruled. "We will send an emissary," the council leader said. "He will ask what Kur wants for ransom."

"Let me go!" Sint volunteered, but was refused.

"Kur would say that you are an escaped captive and would ask another ransom," the leader told him.

Two days went by before the emissary departed with his guard. Sint fretted. "The assembly wastes time. Lugud could be sold into slavery by now."

Many days more passed without a word from the emissary. The harvest season ended; the canals were made strong for the rainy season; the city tended to its affairs.

Sint and Ashna were called to help make a copy of the cart. "That will be dull work," Sint growled. "I would rather go out to seek Lugud."

"I would go!" said Ashna quickly.

"We cannot go. We would be outlawed or put to death if we disobeyed," Sint said.

111

At the temple they found two carpenters making a new cart. The sides were of smooth planks; the front was high and glistened with red paint and gold tracery.

"Where are the discs?" the boy asked.

"We have none as yet," a carpenter told him. "Yours were the simplest to make, but they used end-grain. They split."

"I know that," Ashna admitted. "Do you plan to use boards? Their grain would run at right angles to the roller."

"The boards are too small," the other carpenter said. "We need a very wide board so we can make large discs for good rolling."

"We can use two or three boards." Sint traced a circle in the dust and laid three sturdy planks across it. "We can cut here, and use cross-pieces to hold the disc together and make it strong. It can be larger than the end of the thickest roller."

Made in that way, the new wheels worked better than the old. A handsome temple cart was finished and put on a high place for everyone to see.

Ashna was permitted to take his fast-roller home. Sint helped him to make the new type of wheels for it and

112

gave him the frame of the old sledge for his own.

Night pulled the improved cart easily enough, but there was a limit to its use: the noise still frightened people, and any animals that heard it coming were apt to stampede. Essna told the boy to drive slowly and to use the cart for work and not for play.

Soon the first rainstorm came. "The emissary we sent to Kur is still away," said Sint despondently. "Now every new storm will delay him more."

The family despaired. Ti'amat watched from the window. Essna brooded, and Nin grew pale with worry.

"Lugud might be safe somewhere," Essna said to Nin, but that was only a hope. They all knew that Lugud might be dead — killed in the first attack or in some attempted escape.

"And what of you, Sint, and Ashna?" asked Nin. "All three of you may be called for caravan duty. It becomes more dangerous every year."

Essna had no answer. He put an offering before the shrine and brought the family to the temple for prayer and sacrifice.

As the season wore on, the assembly listened with more attention to Essna and Sint.

113

LUGUD IS CAPTURED

"Something must be done," one official admitted. "It is time for more caravans to go, but the crewmen are afraid."

"Both the Tigris and Euphrates are dangerous in the north," another said. "Could we get supplies from other Sumerian cities in the south?"

"They have their own troubles," said Sint. "They have to get supplies from the north as we do. We must prepare to fight!"

But while they argued, the decision was snatched from them. Soon after the first day of spring, the emissary returned alone. He had been a captive, as some had feared.

"Kur let me go to bring his message," the emissary said. "His warriors cover the plains, for he has many chieftains with him. He holds many Sumerians: Lugud's caravan, my guards, and some who have been slaves for years.

"He says he will decide for himself the amount of ransom. He demands that we open the temple stores to him."

Ashna and the Fast-Roller

11

The assembly was staggered. "Kur does not think that we would submit to that!" the leader cried.

The emissary continued. "If we do not, he will kill his captives, one by one. He says further that he will do this before the city wall where we can see!"

The assembly leader needed no vote; the men stamped and shouted in rage. "We will fight," the leader said. "Let us select a battle leader, one who knows the enemy."

"Sint should lead," someone said. "He has reason to fight well, and he is a tried warrior. He knows the tricks of the tribesmen, and he has calm judgment, even in a battle."

The men yelled in agreement, for many had served with Sint on caravans and knew of his steadiness in time of peril.

"I once voted against Sint's opinions, but I am with him now," one man declared. "Let us make him the battle leader. Let us all vote for him, every one of us, and show him and the city that we are united against Kur!" There was no opposition.

Sint accepted. He made a speech, starting by reminding the assembly that Lugud would have resisted from the beginning. "Kur is like a serpent," he told the assembly. "He knows no law but his own, and he grows so big that he coils around us. Let us resist him and the other bandits at every move lest, like the serpents of our legends, they renew their strength every year. Crush them before they grow. Bring them within the law."

To a Sumerian, a serpent was a living sign of the underworld, and Sint's words threw the assembly into a frenzy of war spirit. It was some time before he could calm them enough to talk of plans for fighting the tribesmen.

"Kur chooses the plain," Sint said. "That is best for us, also. We will let him approach. When he is near enough, I will lead a strong force of mounted men through the main gate. Men on foot will guard the other gates, with the assembly members as captains. The older men and boys will stand on the walls to fend off any assaults there."

The assembly cheered. The plan was clear. Further details were soon settled. Essna would direct the defense in the city itself. He and the other captains would hold their onagers in reserve so that they could ride quickly wherever they were needed, but Sint would have nearly every other mount in the city at his command. When everything was understood, Sint dismissed the assembly.

That same day, Kur was seen on the plain. Inside the gates, the Sumerian force gathered. There were long lines of men and onagers. They waited for orders from Sint.

Some distance north of the canal, the enemy halted. From a place next to Essna atop the wall, Ashna saw the tribesmen raise several black tents. Smoke from their campfires made a dark line against the blue sky.

"Kur takes his time," said Essna angrily.

Ashna saw Sint ride through the ranks of the city forces. "The enemy has taken position," Sint called. "Be ready."

A lookout shouted, "Kur comes this way with a troop of riders."

Sint climbed the wall to see. Everyone watched silently as the troop came near.

Kur halted on the far side of the canal. He shouted something, and beside him a man repeated his message in Sumerian. "Do you know my terms?"

Ashna started. "That little man — I would know him anywhere. He was foreman of the loggers!"

"Kur must have a treaty with him," said Essna. "So the wolves gather from afar when they think a deer has fallen."

Sint was answering even as Essna spoke. "We know your terms. You would slay our brothers unless we surrender. But we do not know that you have them, or that they are alive."

"They are in the tents," the foreman shouted. "We will give you until sundown to make your decision. You are evil people, sorcerers, and magicians. We will give you no longer."

"We do not need that time," said Sint. "Our force equals yours."

Kur roared something to the foreman, and Ashna

heard a man on the wall translate the arrogant words: "It is the Calm One, that caravan leader. He will not fight."

"He means you, Sint," someone said.

"If I were you, I would talk no more," Essna said in a grim tone.

But Sint was climbing down from the wall. He spoke quickly to the throng of Sumerian riders and led them to the gate opening. Ashna heard his final orders. "Ride close together. Hit toward their center. Drive for the tents."

He gave a crisp command. There was a sudden rush of hooves as the Sumerians streamed through the gate.

Kur's onager reared and darted away. His troop retreated a short distance. A moment later, a drum rolled faintly in the camp and other tribesmen joined Kur's troop.

Sint and his riders thudded across the narrow wooden bridges over the canal. Watching, Ashna felt his own hands clench. The forces met head on.

There was a tangle of mounts and riders. Brown dust clouded the plain. Through it came the red, coppery flash of spearhead and dagger, the bray of onagers, the hoarse shouts of men, the thump of the drum.

Abruptly the clamor halted. The tribesmen drew

back, their robes fluttering as they sped to their camp. On the wall, the older men and boys cried out in relief. Some of Sint's men started after the tribesmen, but he summoned them to return.

"Go no farther," Sint warned as they came back. "Kur could draw you into a trap. That was just a test with part of his forces. They wanted to see if we would really fight. Now — see how the others come and spread out."

A horde of tribesmen turned aside from where Sint's warriors clustered, and stopped beyond the city to the east. Some of them dismounted.

"They have digging tools," said Ashna. "What do they think to do?"

Essna stared. "They are breaking in one side of the canal." His eyes were wide in disbelief. "The water will run over the plain. They must be stopped."

Facing the city, other tribesmen rode out from the center to both sides.

"Kur will hit us everywhere at once," someone shouted.

Sint waved his spear. The Sumerians lashed their onagers forward. The forces collided again; riders fell. Neither side would retreat.

On the wall, Essna moved suddenly. "I cannot stand here. I helped to build those canals. While some of the enemy engage Sint, the others begin to wreck the city as if they knew they could not lose."

Essna climbed down. He beckoned to two members of the assembly. "Ride to the south gates. Detach a few men from each place and bring them here. I will call others from the west. We will form a company to defend the canals."

They galloped away. Several boys moved towards the ladders to join the new group, but a temple guard shouted, "Stay where you are. If the enemy gets past Sint, we must defend the city."

"Now they come!" someone yelled in terror. The drum rolled; the tribesmen roared as they closed in around Sint. Some of their cries were understood: "Hurl the Sumerians back — slay them — magicians —sorcerers." The voices were sharp with hate.

Slowly the Sumerians fought their way forward, a closely knit force, driving toward the tents. Around them, the lines of screaming tribesmen bent in to close a vast circle.

Ashna climbed down the wall and ran toward his

house. Nin called to him, and Essna, riding now at the head of a column of men, reined in hard. "Boys are to stay on the wall. Do not run away. You must not shame us."

"I do not run away," Ashna shouted. "The tribesmen think we are sorcerers. That is the battle cry Kur and the foreman use to stir their men. We have sorcery — we should use it!

"The fast-roller frightens everyone. I will bring it to the plain."

Essna's onager pranced in impatience. "It is a brave and manly gesture," Ashna's father said. He glanced back as the battle noise rose furiously. "But we do not ask that boys risk their lives." He whipped the onager and dashed for the gate.

Ashna ran into the stable and harnessed Night to the cart. Nin had joined some others on the wall. But Ti'amat was there to help. "Bring Lugud back!" she said earnestly. "Oh, I wish girls could go!"

Ashna threw his weapons on the cart and climbed up. He called to Night, and the sturdy little onager lunged forward. The wheels spun.

Near the gate Ashna saw the company gathered, with Essna at their head.

The cart squealed to a stop. The onagers nearby shied away. "Go back," Essna snapped. "You frighten them."

"That is it — I could frighten the tribesmen and their onagers," Ashna said quickly. His own fear was that Essna might repeat the command and that he would be bound to obey.

"Get the other cart from the temple," he pleaded. "Come with me. You are the only one who would know what to do with the other fast-roller. The two would sound together like the Voice of Enlil."

Essna hesitated. "They think we are magicians," Ashna begged.

His father nodded. "Take this company," he shouted to one of the captains. "Stand ready to follow me when I return." He plunged through the crowd toward the temple. Ashna waited anxiously. Through the gate he could see the battle and hear the cries of the wounded.

Sint's gallant men fought their way through the mob of tribesmen. Arrows rained down. The circle slowly closed around the Sumerians.

Far down the dusty street came the squeal of the temple cart as Essna got it moving. It was the sound

Ashna waited for. He lashed the reins. Night trotted forward. Ashna caught a glimpse of Essna drawing abreast of him, and he shouted at Night. "Run, run!"

The colt galloped. The wheels squealed and shrieked. Essna's onager was nearly wild with fear at the sound of

THE FIRST WHEEL

the temple cart behind him, and he raced forward too.

The Sumerian force was far ahead. The enemy circling them was nearer. Ashna guided Night that way. He put the reins in one hand and with the other picked up his spear.

ASHNA AND THE FAST-ROLLER

His cart shrieked toward the tribesmen. The nearest enemy stopped. His mount pawed the air, threw him off, and fled across the plain. The tribesman screamed in fear and flung himself away from the oncoming wheels.

A second enemy onager bolted. Others brayed in terror. Several plunged into the canal to escape.

Far down the plain, the arrogant tribesmen with the digging tools looked up as Essna's cart careened toward them with the company of foot soldiers following at a full run. Their faces twisted with fear. They fled. Essna got control of his terrified onager and guided it around toward Ashna.

The boy pointed. Essna guessed what he meant: they would frighten the onagers of their own men if they came too close. Together the two carts whirled wide around the flank of Sint's group, toward the tents.

The Sumerians were not long in understanding what had happened. Better disciplined than the nomad horde, they listened to the commands of their officers, drew to one side, then closed in after the carts.

The crude war chariots dashed among the tents. The guards scattered in confusion, leaving behind all the captive Sumerians, and the captives set up a great shout of

126

welcome. Ashna and Essna heard Lugud's roaring voice in the tumult, and they hurried to free him.

Across the plain, Kur and his men fled in wild disorder. Most were now on foot, for their terrified onagers had thrown them and were racing in a stampede.

Sint ordered two groups to capture the tribesmen on foot and to run down their onagers. Then he dismounted and joined Ashna. Lugud and the others were pale and thin but unharmed. Essna was trying to explain Ashna's action with the carts.

"I heard them," Mashkim said. "I am still shaking. I thought that Enlil himself was coming."

Essna said with satisfaction, "Enlil and Enzu look upon us with favor, for we have won a great victory. Kur's strength is broken."

"There is something of the gods in those discs." Sint stared at the carts. "If I did not know how they were made, I, too, might have fled."

"There is wisdom in the discs." Essna put his hand proudly on Ashna's shoulder. "And here is wisdom and courage in a boy. Ashna, your fast-roller has saved the city."

"Let me ride home with you," Lugud said wearily.

He climbed onto Ashna's cart. Several of the other captives followed.

"Not me," said Mashkim superstitiously. "Not on one of those things. I will walk."

The Sumerians turned back to their city, and the screeching chariots led the way.